THIS LITTLE TIGER BOOK BELONGS TO:

_____

_____

_____

_____

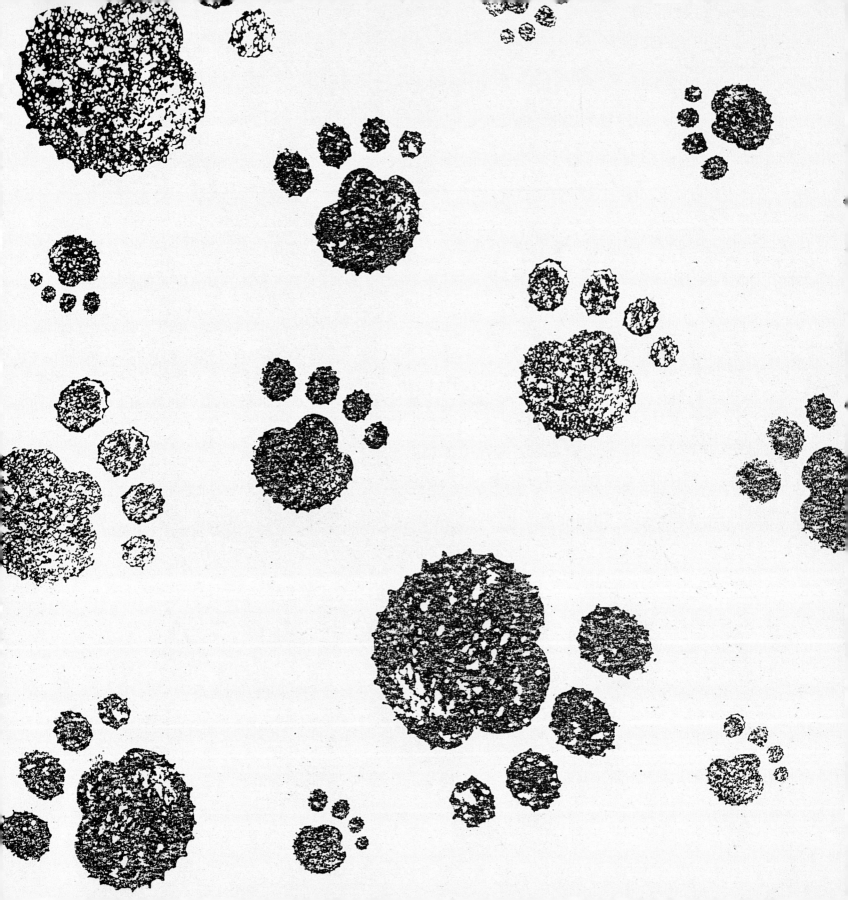

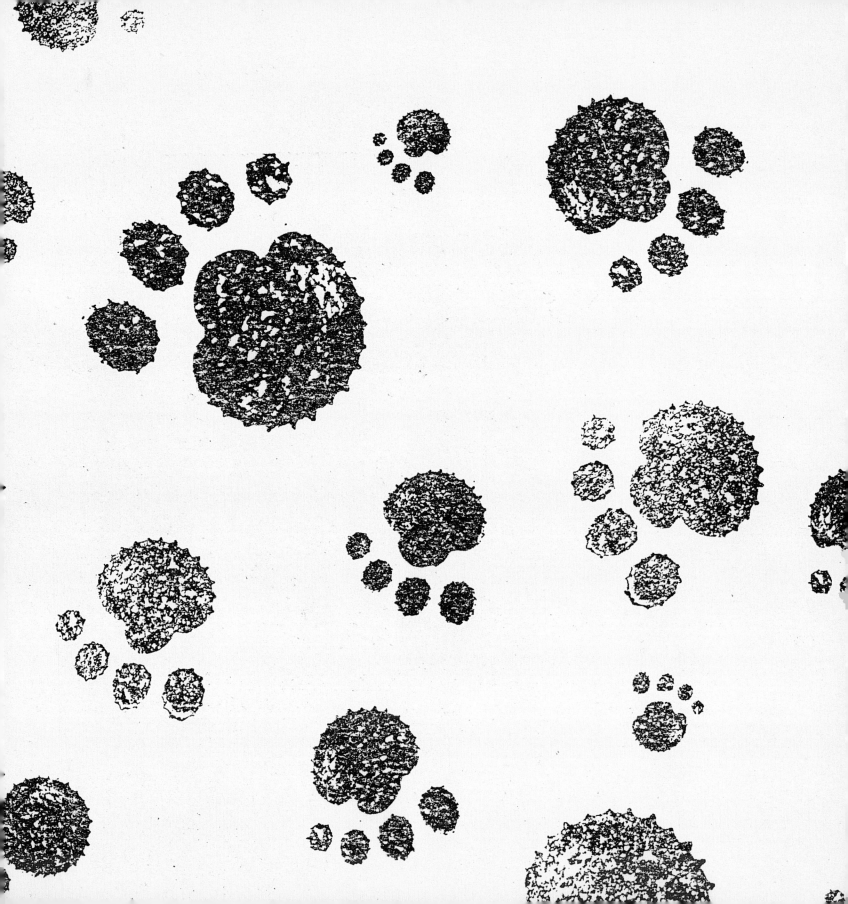

For Krystyna
—L.J.

For Lucy & Sophie
—C.J.C.

LITTLE TIGER PRESS
An imprint of Magi Publications,
1 The Coda Centre, 189 Munster Road, London SW6 6AW
This paperback edition published 1999 · First published in Great Britain 1999
Text © 1999 Linda Jennings · Illustrations © 1999 Caroline Jayne Church
Linda Jennings and Caroline Jayne Church have asserted their rights to be
identified as the author and illustrator of this work under the Copyright,
Designs and Patents Act, 1988.
Printed in Singapore · All rights reserved · ISBN 1 84143 004 8
3 5 7 9 10 8 6 4 2

Nine Naughty Kittens

by Linda Jennings & Caroline Jayne Church

LITTLE TIGER PRESS
London

One
wobbly kitten,
after something
new . . .

Two

Kitten meets
another one,
and then there
are . . .

Three frightened
kittens,
peeping round
the door . . .

Four

"Boo!" says little Ginger, and then there are . . .

Five furry
kittens
find a
pile of
sticks...

Jasper's
sleeping
under them,
and then
there are . . .

Six sniffing kittens find a fishy heaven. . .

Seven silly kittens try to climb a gate . . .

jump upon
another kitten,
then there
are . . .

Eight

Eight
eager kittens,
walking in a
line . . .

Nine naughty kittens
find a cosy
den . . .

"Come to me,"
says Mother Cat,
and then there
are . . .

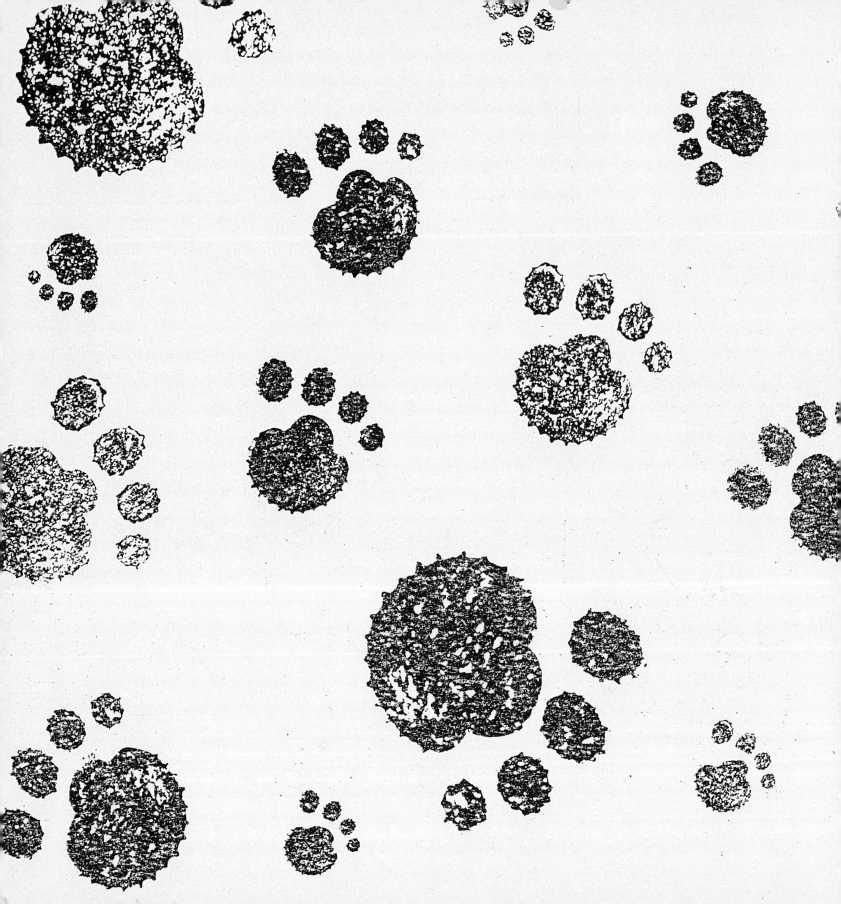

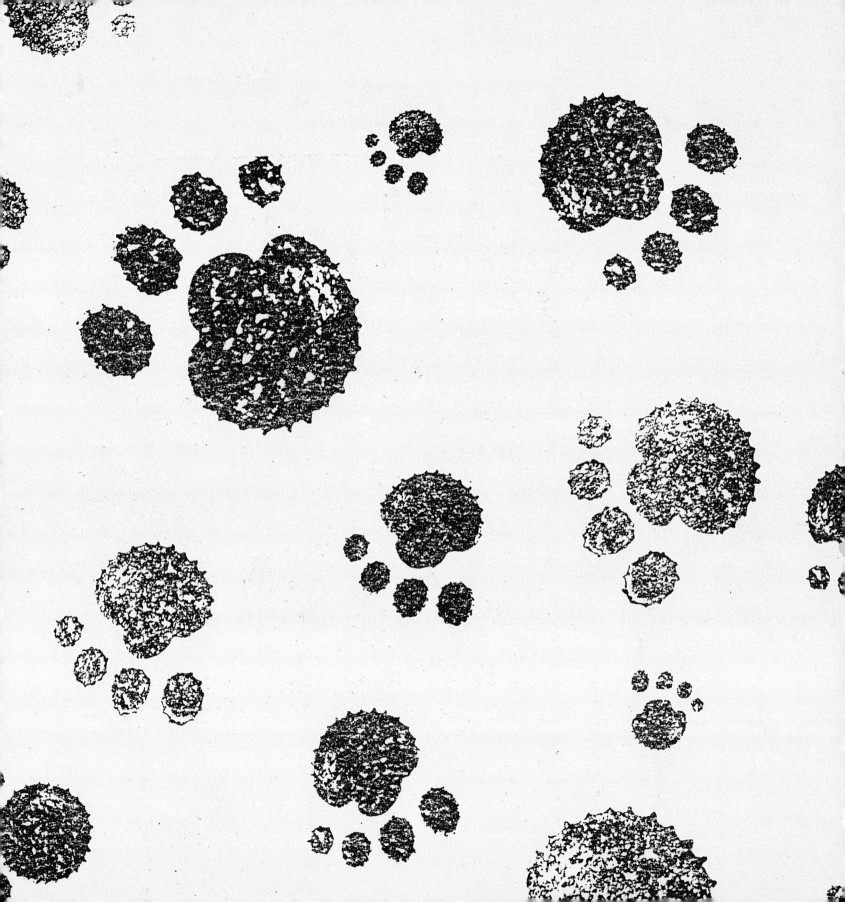

Join the LITTLE TIGER CLUB now for lots more books to enjoy!

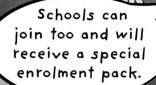

Schools can join too and will receive a special enrolment pack.

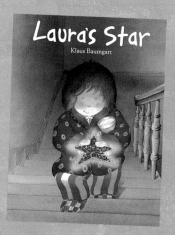
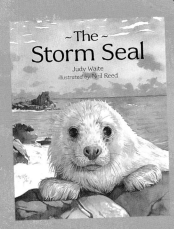

Join the LITTLE TIGER CLUB now and receive a special Little Tiger goody bag containing badges, pencils and more! Once you become a member you will be sent details of special offers, competitions and news of new books. Why not write a book review? The best reviews will be published on book covers or in the Little Tiger Press catalogue.

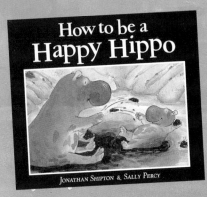

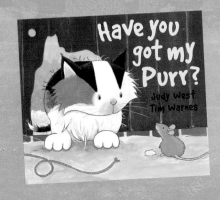
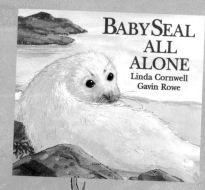